After the Heroin:
A Mother's Story in Poetry

Susan Mitchell

Old Seventy Creek Press
Albany, Kentucky

OLD SEVENTY CREEK PRESS

COPYRIGHT 2017 BY **Susan Mitchell**

2017 OLD SEVENTY CREEK FIRST EDITION

PRINTED IN THE UNITED STATES OF AMERICA
ALL RIGHTS RESERVED UNDER INTERNATIONAL
AND PAN-AMERICAN COPYRIGHT CONVENTIONS

PUBLISHED IN THE UNITED STATES
BY OLD SEVENTY CREEK PRESS
RUDY THOMAS, PUBLISHER
P. O. BOX 204
ALBANY, KENTUCKY 42602

ISBN-10: 0-9982374-8-5
EAN-13: 978-0-9982374-8-0

Edited by Anne Shelby

Cover Picture by Susan Mitchell

For Reuben

"Trade sorrow for a page"

— Ernest Hemingway, (*88 Poems*)

Contents

After the Heroin:
A Mother's Story in Poetry

Introduction

"We found your son's body," the assistant coroner said through the phone. "It looks like he died of a heroin overdose. " These are words no parent ever wants to hear. I sat in the car, pulled to the side of the road, on my way to my son, Reuben's, home an hour away.

It had been a long struggle for Reuben. The addiction took hold of him more than a decade ago when he was 13. He had been to three rehab centers in three different cities. Reuben had been clean two years this time. He was engaged and would be married in two months when he accidentally overdosed. His roommate found him on the floor of his basement bedroom.

So, instead of going to Reuben's home, his dad and I met his fiancée at the coroner's office. We could see Reuben there. We talked to the coroner and the assistant for a while, answered questions as best we could before they let us see him. They told us he would be behind a glass window and we could stay as long as we needed to stay. I asked if I could touch Reuben. They said no. It was against policy.

We walked down the hall toward the window. There he was, covered with a paper sheet up to his neck. All we could see was his face and head. The atmosphere was cold, sterile. So unlike Reuben's normal jovial personality.

I looked at him and willed him to open his eyes and talk to me. I wanted to hear his voice, look into his eyes. I wanted to hug him until he woke up. I wanted this to be a dream I would wake from or a mistake that someone had made. But it wasn't and I would never hug him again. My one and only child was gone.

We had his viewing the Sunday before Mother's Day. The funeral director estimated that nearly 1000 people came to Reuben's viewing and funeral. Reuben would have been happy to know so many people came.

Almost every day there is a story on the news about the heroin problem and what measures are being taken to combat it. Heroin is affordable and accessible. It is killing too many of our children. Reuben was 23 years old when he died in 2014, but he was still my child.

While this book is raw, it is real and shows the love I have for my son even when he was actively using. I did not like what the drugs did to him and it put us through the most challenging times of our lives.

This book is for all the parents, siblings, wives, husbands, sons, daughters, families and friends who are dealing with addiction in some way every day. It is also for recovering addicts so they can see what someone who loves an addict has gone through while they were using. I have written poems throughout the first year after Reuben's death about my thoughts and emotions including one that was written when he was using. These are challenging to read, but they were necessary for me to write in order to keep my sanity. My hope is that these poems will help you deal with your own emotions as you deal with whatever addiction or loss is affecting your own life.

Acknowledgments

Thank you to all therapists, acupuncturists, and other medical staff who work with addicts day after day, especially those who are recovering addicts themselves. You give us time with our loved ones we would not have without your care. I cherish every day you gave me with Reuben.

Thank you to all my friends, too numerous to name, who supported me during all the times when Reuben was using, the times when he wasn't and after he died. I love you so much and appreciate all of you.

Thank you to my family who listen to me when I cry, hear me when I vent, sit in my silence, read my poetry, calm my nerves, make me laugh. During the year after Reuben's death, after I was diagnosed with cancer, Mom and Peggy drove me to doctor's appointments, chemotherapy, grocery, pharmacy, and anywhere I wanted to go. Jennifer and Mom listened to my rants and my words when I missed Reuben and could do nothing about it.

Thank you to Judy Sizemore for being kind enough to read all the poetry I send to you and encouraging me to write through whatever is happening in my life. Thank you for helping me to see that I am an artist and for giving me the opportunities to prove it.

Getting Clean was first published in Directionally Challenged (But Finding My Way Home) Old Seventy Creek Press 2014.

Beginning Again will appear in **Lady!** Magazine in

June 2017

For Me to Survive

the best thing I can do is write. It is the safest thing.
I imagine a magnificent manuscript that could
whisper to people, say their names, call to them,
provide comfort, share moments, understand.
I can only write what I know. I can only process
what I have experienced. I can only share what
I have.

Generosity is wide and travels beyond boundaries
to encompass anyone who might benefit from the
despair of others. One person's pain could be a
teachable moment for others and save the life of
someone loved. *post traumatic growth*

I do not believe the number of people
who die is as important as who the people are.
It was my son.
It just takes one for me.

His War

I want the world to know my son's struggle
and how he tried with all his might
to conquer that which enveloped him.
Addiction is a brutal demon that, at its weakest,
pours acid on the soul.
At its strongest, rages battles
against everyone it touches
until we all fall prey
and lose the power to sustain life itself.

A person who truly fights
their addiction wages a war within themselves,
their families and society.
They must win them all, on some level, to succeed.
Each twenty four hours begins another battle
that they must win.

My son's battle raged every day
for the last full decade of his young life.
He succumbed to a disease
as deadly and as dangerous as any war
we could ever wage.

Addiction

is the piece of a story pushed
through a syringe into the
vein of someone who right
now doesn't remember
the first chapter
and tomorrow
won't want to
read the
book
again

Being Safe

A woman told me her grandchildren were in Texas
with their dad. She had not seen them in three days.
She smiled, said this was the longest time she had been
away from them. She did not know if she could take it
until the end of the week when they come home.

Today is day 63 since I have seen my son. Tomorrow
will be day 64. Every new day will be the longest time
since I have spoken to him.

I can hear him in my thoughts. I saved days of texting
back and forth with him. He told me he loved me.
I texted back, "I know." He replied, "Good."

He worked at night. Sometimes before I went to bed
I texted him to ask how work was going, tell him I loved
him, tell him goodnight. I would say, "Be safe."
He assured me he would.

One night he did not respond. He did not call.
That was the night he stopped being safe.

Getting Clean

I lay across the floor
scrubbing dirt only I can see,
so close to my face
I cannot miss it.
Dirt, like the drugs filling my son's
body, filling in the memory
lapses like blackness in grout.

I scrub until my fingers ache.
I wipe the liquid charcoal from his lips.

He asks the same question
over and over again,
the same one I ask the floor
as I stare at the suds and puddles,
"How did I get here?"

We were together most of his
life. Just the two of us.
We played in the park,
ate ice cream.
I gave him his first puppy.
He named the mutt Tony.
I never knew why.

Now I smell the lemon-fresh
scent of my kitchen floor,
counters, mirrors, sink,
shower, toilet.

be her way of coping

How did I get here?

I remember watching him
as he unfastened his seat belt
to get out of the car
and walk into school by himself,
knowing someday he would walk
into places I had not taken him.
I never imagined it would be
this place.

I dip the brush deep into the bucket
as if answers had settled to the bottom.
Steam rises like smoke from a bong
in a room filled with people
I would never invite into my home.

I tell my son his black tongue
reminds me of our dog Sam
with the purple tongue.
"How did I get here?" he asks.

We used to walk across the huge
lawn of a nearby church every Friday
on our way to pick up a pizza.
In the dusk he ran ahead and
lay down in the grass, "Mommy,
can you find me?"
I always could.

I hold the Styrofoam cup so

he can drink more of the liquid
designed to save a life.
He looks at me with eyes that
shake too much for him to
see me and I cannot find him.
How did we get here?

My kitchen floor has puddles
as if the rain had come in,
a muddy, dirty rain.

I dip the mop in fresh, clean
water, twist it until the excess
runs back where it came from.
I envision my son's dealer,
my hands wrapped around
his throat
twisting,
twisting.

signs of anger about the situation

I mop up the water,
empty the bucket,
lay exhausted on the couch.

My home is fresh and clean.

*night time
is when all the
thoughts get mixed
up*

Bombs

Maybe it is

because of the

darkness

or the

quiet

or the

solitude.

Whatever the reason,

night time

is the most

unforgiving.

Thoughts

fall

like

bombs

all

around

me

and I cannot find you

anywhere.

Saying Hello

He leaned against the bedroom
wall, this young man looking for

his place in the world, in this room.
Heroin coursed through his veins,

like drunken race cars.
He picked up his phone

and dialed a number he knew—
Mom's.

The heroin was on a crash course
with his body, his mind.
It was different this time.

The voicemail answered.
"I can't come to the phone right now..."

He could not finish his message.
It was a slurred hello but time

mixed with the poison in his veins
did not let him finish.

He tried to catch himself as his
body collapsed on the

concrete floor

covered in carpet.

Mom wondered why the message
was incomplete.

She called him again and again.
Her calls went unanswered.

Forever.

A Time for Tea

Light from the window make
their faces look like watches
with broken hands and no
time to stop what they are
doing, to rewind to the time
when all this began, and

might be turned around.
It isn't what you think:
It is life as people live it.
Bodies sitting at a table
at dusk drinking chamomile
tea trying to drink in the idea

that their son just died.
Nothing can stop it now.
If time could stop they would make
it happen. If they could make
everything go away, they would.
So they sit and sip a

no parent should have to do this

calming concoction while
steeping in pallid thoughts.
Tomorrow is so far away.
Plans will have to be made
with his wishes in mind.
All thoughts will circle around

a son who cannot attend

the final day meant for him – A
farewell party with a missing host.
But today his parents cannot
speak, cannot cry, They sit
in the evening twilight

staring at their stark white cups or
the dull and lifeless sunset
not caring that if they sit all night,
when dawn comes, the only thing
that will have changed is that
their tea will have grown cold.

Georgia

Georgia grieved for him. She had lain
beside him all night on that last night.
She could not call anyone for help so
she lay pressed against him for comfort,
from him or for him no one knows.

They had played and wrestled
together with such exuberance. They took
naps together with his arm draped over her,
her body against his.

We got special permission for
Georgia to attend the funeral.
When it was time to go to the church,
she sat down obediently so the
leash could be attached to her collar.
She walked into the church proud
and quiet. At the casket, she put her
front paws on its hand rail and peered in.
There he was, but this time his eyes did not
 twinkle and he did not call her to him
so he could stroke her hair and pat her rib cage.

No, today he was silent as the last time
they were together. Georgia looked at him
as long as she could, then lay on the floor,
stretched full length as she had during their naps,
as she had that last night. And Georgia cried.

A dog without
it's owner

What to Say

The suddenness of death,
no matter how quick or long it takes,
is always a surprise.
We knew my dad was sick and,
although he had been in the hospital the
first five days of May, it was
a shock when the call came –
the finality of it. Death is absolute,
there are no maybes.
The future on Earth no longer exists.
Everyone else stays here and wonders:
What happens now? How can I continue?
Who's next?
Questions beginning with Why are never
answered and are useless to ask
but still they linger on the tips of our
tongues, in the backs of our minds.
When the anger comes – and it will—
Why is the first question asked,
often in a scream or followed by sobs
that shake the soul.

Right now I have no questions. My mind *shock numbness*
is an empty, echoing warehouse where pigeons
nest and light streams in through dirty windows.
Inside myself, I am heavy.
My soul is clad in lead.
The exterior of me looks the same as always –
same skin, same eyes, same hair.

My demeanor is off.

I do not know how to respond to people.
I say *thank you* often and I mean it.
I do not know what else to say.
I want to talk about him but he
is private inside me. He is mine.
He is my child. I want to protect
the essence, the memory, the life of him.

I do not know how.

With Every Needle Stick

Heroin shot through his veins and wrapped
itself around his heart and, like acid,
dissolved the love he had for his fiancé,
his mom, his aunt, his grandmother, his dad, his friends.

The coroner said one moment he was
alive and the next moment he wasn't.
It almost sounded like he had not
suffered, but he had. A decade

of addiction, recovery, amends.
His soul twisting and turning with every
needle stick, every pill. This disease ate
away the person he was until he was

the person he had become. Some say it
is a voluntary disease. It is as
voluntary as breathing, but he could
only hold his breath for so long. He needed

everyone needs help in times of trouble

support, someone to help pump oxygen
into his lungs when the drugs made him
forget how to inhale on his own. He
hid his secret well. He had a decade

of practice and had mastered deception.
No one knew how long he had not breathed
until he stopped all together. Then the
heroin cursed through all our veins as if

we held the needle ourselves. His blood flowed
in our veins but we did not feel the high,
just the crash of coming down. The crash of
losing someone who had lost himself. Now

his struggles lay on our shoulders, not
because he put them there, but because we
are all second guessing how we could have
stopped this horrible ending. He would have

what they could have done differently?

told us, there was nothing we could say or
do if he did not want help. Now there is
nothing anyone can say or do that
will help any of us. The syringes

have been emptied, the pills ingested. He
made arrangements to get drugs, then we made
arrangements for him. That is how it works.
I am not a better person because

I have never shot heroin into
my body. I am a better person
for having known and loved the young man
who grieved as much for us before
we knew how much we would grieve for him.

After the Heroin

What do you do after the heroin --
when the needle has pierced the skin
and dangles from your arm?
When the words you wanted to say
fall on the floor beside you,
shattering into a million unspoken syllables?

What do you do when the anger is gone,
the high never came and you wish
you could make that one phone call for help
to someone who would have come?

How can you stop the phone call to your Mom?
The one where the coroner says, "We found
your son's body".   How can you answer her
when she stands at the glass window
separating your cold body from her warm one,
and she whispers to you,
"Talk to me, please talk to me"?

What do you do after the heroin –
when you can no longer hide what you have done?
Toxicology tells what you did, not
what you meant to do.
Just a little to get you by becomes
time of death.

After the heroin, your mom tucks you in
in your nice black suit. Your fiancée kisses

your forehead with raisin colored lipstick,
just enough to piss you off.
But you have no way of cleaning off your forehead,
as they had no way of cleaning out your veins.

Bad Batch

Administrator. Administratrix. Executor.
Executrix. Titles all of them.
My son has died.
I need no title to feel this pain deep
within my soul.

I am assigned his property to sell
and pay his funeral expenses. Beyond
this world he is paying his own debts
with the little he owned.
Others should chip in.

The dealer, who thought my son had
gotten "a bad batch". Is there
such a thing as a good batch?
His coworkers who knew and did not speak up.
The friends who did not condone but made it okay.

Me for not paying more attention.
Me for not stepping in and saying, again,
This is enough.
He would tell me this was no one's fault but his own.
He made the choice. He bought, cooked,

snorted, popped, injected of his own free will.
Strangers shake their heads. He was just one more
addict. Tsk, tsk. Another statistic.
I want to scream *he is not a statistic*. He was loved.
He had value. He was special to many. He was sick.

[handwritten margin notes: always the question of what they could have done differently]

But my voice is drowned by the sirens of someone else needing the help my son did not receive in time.

That Silence

Drugs searched him out
and tugged at his shirt sleeve. *"Pick me,*
pick me" they whispered. The whisper
became a wail. The voice quieted when
he swallowed pills. It was silent when
he put the needle in his arm. And when
the high came crashing down, it laughed.

we all have addictions
that consume our lives; food, technology,
drugs, alcohol, sex, porn

Drowning in Dawn

I am underwater. I hold my breath,
kick my feet and make angelic ripples
in the water. It is not a swimming pool,
river, or ocean. It is a cylindrical, plexi-glass
tank and people on the outside stare
at me as if I am an ugly fish
they have never seen before.

when the loss happens, people look at you to see your reaction and then never help, just stare

My scales drop off like dead skin
and float to the surface. The gathering crowd
make faces and back away
from this hideous creature in the water.

I tap on the sides of the cylinder,
begging silently for someone
to let me out. My lungs begin to burn.
I try to swim upward to get some air
but the water is too deep
and I am too weak. Finally,
I take that involuntary gulp of air,
only it is not air, but the water and floating debris.
I realize this is how people drown. I flail my arms
and gasp as I inhale more water
that goes directly to my lungs.
Just as the world goes black.
I gasp again and sit straight up on my bed
in the real world.
I look around me and see no water.
But the blackness itself surrounds me still.

This is how my day begins.

every day is a never ending
fight against the sadness (darkness)

Masked

I rubbed clay on my face this morning
and formed new lips that smiled
so friendly. My eyebrows raised
as if I was ready to laugh. I drew crow's feet
beside both eyes to make them look less flat.

I breathed deep as I walked down
the hall to my desk, legs as unsteady
as wet rolled out clay.
Under this earthen façade
there was nothing.
I greeted coworkers as though life
was normal, my family intact.

But it did not take long for my mask
to dry and crack. The tears
flowed under the clay
until it fell in chunks to the floor.
My dirty face, swollen eyes
and smile-less lips uncovered
and grotesque as a new grave.

Future

My attention span is as
short as my fuse which is
the length of my hair. So
is my concentration.
My sadness hides behind
anger and frustration.
So that the latter is all
you see.

I see a world that is caving
in upon me, chunks of atmosphere
falling quickly and aiming adeptly.
I dodge crackling clouds and leap
over dysfunctional moons.
I glance at calm stars and wonder
if that is the future I somehow lost.

Searching

My son has died. But I know
he is still here.

I look for him in crowds,
in Michigan,
when I am alone.

He eludes me.

My mind shouts,
calling out to him.
I know he can hear me.
Why isn't he answering?

I talk to him but he does not respond.

All I hear is the cry of the wind,
the splatter of rain,
the deafening quiet of snow.

I search for him in sidewalk cafes,
at the movie theatre,
in the park near the duck pond.

He will be home on his birthday,
at Christmas,
on Wednesday.

Today is Tuesday. I can't wait to see him.

Illusion

He stands before me, an illusion
that comes only at night.
He startles me awake
and stands close enough to touch
me which, if he did, would reach
into the depth of midnight
and rip the scream
right out of me. I lay still and wait
for it to happen. Instead, he points
toward the window
as if there is a story
there that he cannot tell.
I look but see nothing.
He keeps his head
turned away from me
so I do not know him. He is small
like a child with straight black hair
so I know he is not a vision of you.
I do not know him
and yet he stands there
in his white, white skin
and red t-shirt pointing
at something, I know not what.
I lay there watching him,
he who has light upon him
in a room full of darkness.
Soon, despite the fear, I fall asleep,
hoping, in daylight,
he will be gone.

No More Room

I have no more room for death.
My soul lay beside the grave
weeping, becoming one with the
grass and rain.

My carcass walks around as if
life still exists and the sun
has the right to fall upon me.

I am not embalmed so I
continue to decay from the
inside. When my organs
no longer exist, my skin and
bones will follow until
my shoes are empty,
found in mid-step on the ground.

A janitor, the undertaker of
garbage, will come along, sweep
them up and bury them
in a cylindrical aluminum casket.

I will need no funeral
or headstone.
I will lie beside the grave
near my soul and dissolve
until I am sharing a pillow
with the person who knows
I have no more room for death.

Mourning Walk Through the Cemetery

A nonjudgmental line below the
date of birth and death fills space
on a headstone.

Gone Fishing. Gone but not forgotten.
Sorry I couldn't stay. Frugal epitaphs to
help a loved one rest well.

If no one cared, there would be no granite pillars
to announce their arrival in their new home.
Death is celebrated by well-manicured plots
and flowers on Memorial Day.

Tears falling to the ground quench the thirst
of those six feet below.
At some point the tears dry up, but by then
the casket has become all they need
and there is no thirst for more.

In time we will all rest well.

Universe

His soul was never changed
by the heroin he used.
It kept its quiet power and
projected itself via kindness
when he was clean.
When his body, his soul's Universe,
was clean it could stretch its colorful
wings and fly. His eyes were bright
and his smile quick.
The future was forming in his mind
and was still under construction
when he bought his final dose.
His own Universe did not
see the future come to fruition.
It is the Universe's loss.

Where Do You Go at Night?

Where do you go at night?
Are you whispering to whippoorwills
or finding out the identity of who
is knocking on Owl's door?

Do you watch the young children
as they grow during sleep
and wake up in pajamas too small?

Do you steal socks from dryers
and laugh at the owners as they
search through clothes, dancing
that cold foot dance?

Are you beside my bed, waiting
for the time to hold up the sun,
when you can put the moon away,
then kiss me before I wake so
I do not have to say goodbye again?

Can I Borrow You, My Son?

Can I borrow you, my son?
Borrow you from Death itself so we can continue
our nightly talks of life, love, work, and nothingness?
I have questions for you:
Is Death for real? Must it be permanent?

Can I borrow you?
I want to sit beside you and learn what you know.
I want to apologize for not trusting your friend
who wanted to take you places you'd never been
then loosening the reins for the friends who took
you to places you never should have gone.

Can I borrow you, my son?
You have been in my womb
and felt my heart beat even
before I knew you could feel.
Can you see what I am doing and how much I
weep because you are gone? *Is this what you wanted?*

Can I visit you?
I just want to see where you live now,
understand why the clouds do what they do
and how the stars can stay so still.
I will tell the world it was just a dream
and that you did not put your hand on
my shoulder to guide me through your world.
I will leave quietly and say I never came.

Can I borrow you?
Is Death so malicious that you cannot pause
in your circumstance to talk with me?
Can I borrow you for all time so I never

> have to ask you this again?

She wants him back

Limits

Why does the sky have to be
the limit?
I know you are in the
clouds above me.
Your curious mind will continue
to seek out the new and interesting.
If you can see it, you will
explore the universe. Should
you find another, you will go
there, too.
So, my son, for you, the sky
is not the limit. <u>You are</u>
<u>finally in a space where you</u>
<u>have no limits at all.</u>
<u>Be yourself.</u>

you can be whoever you want b/c there is no judgment

Remains of Wisdom

What does a mother do with the wisdom
she'd planned to share with her son,
and the years she'd planned to spend watching,
to see if he'd understood.

What can she do
when he dies first
with the wisdom she could have given
only to him?

There is no one to whom she may
pass on family traditions, culture.
No child to listen to
her stories. There is no one
Interested in her past.

To whom can she tell
When dealing with a problem always start
with a pleasant tone.

Don't start the fight but defend yourself honorably.

Don't pick on people smaller than you.
Pick on the bigger people picking on the smaller ones.

This gift she wants and needs to share
with her boy who had just become a man
lies dormant in her heart-- dust and ashes.
Wisdom is now the remains

that cannot be scattered across the sea.

She stands on the cliff above the sea,
the wind in chaos, the urn in her hands.
She tilts the urn and the dust of what she
wanted to tell him flies over her and is
carried away by an uncaring wind.

I Imagine Grandchildren

I imagine beautiful children
who crawl up on my lap
so I can read them a book.
I hug them and erase the
mistakes I made the first time.
This generation will be different.
The children will be different.
My intent will be the same:
to do the best I can.

[handwritten annotation: imagining her grandchildren & what she would do differently w/ them]

I imagine my son wrapped
around his daughter's finger
as he wraps his arms around her.
I imagine his son, a new version of
himself with the same silly sense of humor.
I imagine myself a better grandparent
than parent. As a parent, I lacked the
ability to keep my son away from
the dangers of the world.

But, it was in his DNA when he was conceived
to be drawn to pills and needles and
whatever took him beyond his current
state of happiness then drop him into
a hell of his own.
Twelve steps were not enough
for him. He needed thirty-six.
His world became better afterward.
He was in love, he slid a ring

on the finger of the woman who
made him want to be in this world
and not the other. He had beautiful plans.

I imagine grandchildren, one more branch
on the family tree. I have always had a lively
imagination.

Beginning Again

Furniture, boxes, my very breath lay
in an SUV, its back door a mouth open
wide as if gasping for air.
There is a sofa on my shoulders
and spider webs on my tongue. Those who

provided the muscle during this undertaking
smile, proud of accomplishing a tremendous
feat: moving everything left of my life
in three hours.

I step back into the apartment, see what
remains. This part of life is
moving much faster than I prefer.
I wish the world could stop,
give me back my son and

let me meander through the city of
This Won't Happen to Me
the rest of my days.
I don't like being shoved into

It Just Happened Anyway
without a passport. I hear Customs is difficult
to go through when you have no ID.
Maybe, I could take a plane and
ask them to drop me off in

I Don't Want to be Here Anymore.
I hear the weather is hot, mosquitos
are relentless and I will not like it there.
Someone calls to me from outside.

It is time to go.
Time to take the last load
before the rain begins,
then off to get pizza in *Let's Pretend
to Celebrate a Job Well Done.*

Day to Night

Gently, gently make your way into this day.
The dew has barely evaporated from the
morning glories. Step lightly upon grass blades
beneath your feet. Even the dawn is not
sure of what the day will bring.

Clouds buffer the sun from ground and pillow
the world in gentle sorrow.
We cannot fight what fate has brought
but challenge the day to end with comfort.

Night brings what it has to offer. The moon
guides the slumber of those whose eyes
will close forever and softly lights the way
for those who try to reach them.

In the glorious hour before dawn and at the
end of night there is an exchange of
apologies. One for what has happened
and one for what may.

The stars are the tear drops for the end
of something past and the gratitude for what
is to come.

Other books by Susan J. Mitchell

Snapshots takes you on a walk that becomes a journey into yourself, asking questions and making observations that gently awaken the spirit in each of us. The beautiful, artful pictures help readers to see what they may be overlooking in their own lives… We are all, in fact, in the midst of our own amazing "snapshot."

Directionally Challenged knows where it's going. The poems flow from gentle observations of people, beauty and the world to cancer, infidelity, and drug abuse then on to a touching goodbye to a beloved family member. Directionally Challenged will take you places. Open it up and enjoy the ride.

Made in the USA
Lexington, KY
21 August 2017